Munson

Georgia Bulldogs

Munson

Georgia Bulldogs

A Dog Named Munson Finds the Missing Game Ball

Request for permission to make copies of any part of this work should be submitted online at info@mascotbooks.com or mailed to Mascot Books, 560 Herndon Parkway #120, Herndon, VA 20170

PRT0513D

Fourth Printing, May, 2013

Printed in the United States

ISBN-13: 9781620860540
ISBN-10: 1620860546

www.mascotbooks.com

A Dog Named Munson
Finds the Missing Game Ball

Written by
Charlene Thomas

Illustrated by
Laurie Repetto

The Georgia Bulldogs
have a big game on Saturday
... but
the game ball is lost.
The team needs help to find it.

The Bulldogs call their friend
Munson, the golden retriever,
to find the missing
game ball.

Munson goes to the Arch.

Munson goes to the coliseum.

Munson sees the
Redcoat Band practicing.

Munson goes to Foley Field.

Munson goes to
Butts-Mehre to look
in the trophies.

Let's ask Hairy Dawg.

Does Hairy have the game ball ?

NO !

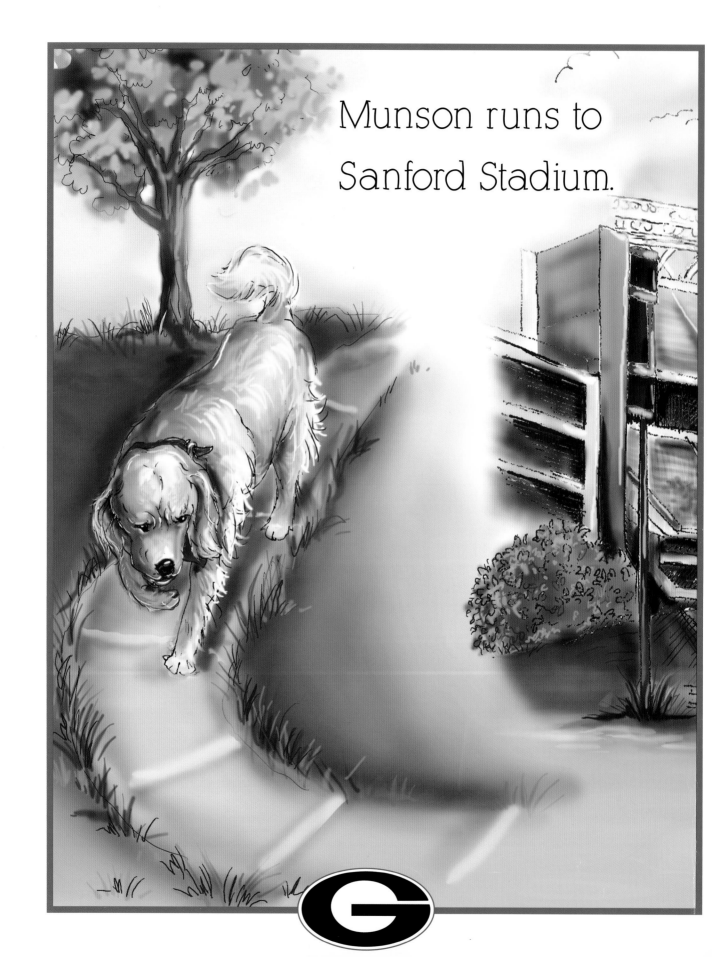

Munson runs to Sanford Stadium.

Munson looks in Uga's dog house.

Now the Bulldogs can play football.

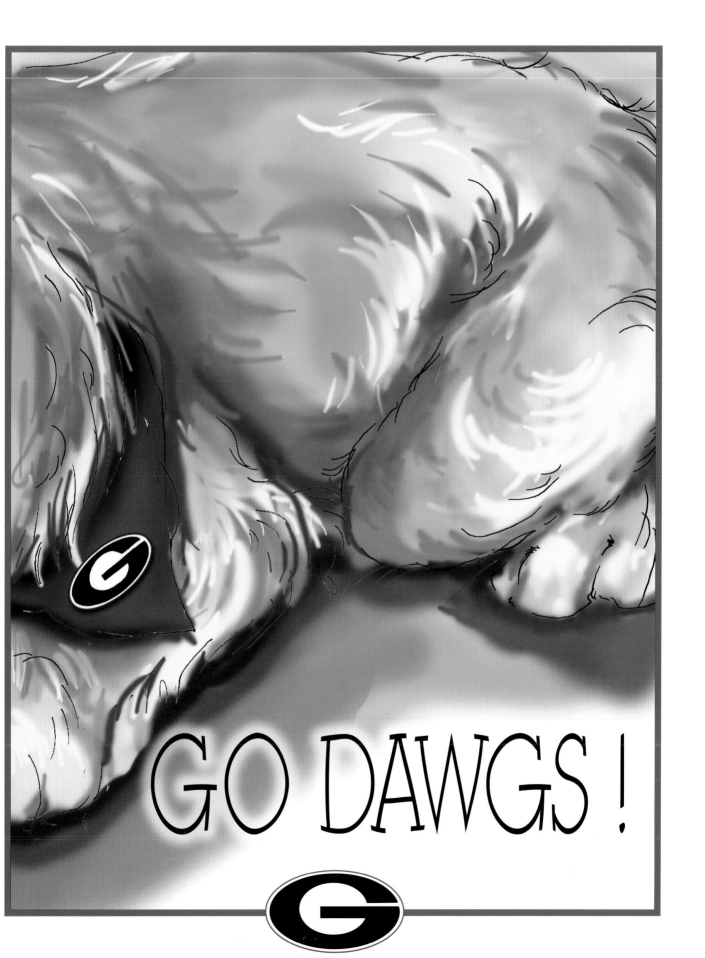

Dedicated to the next generation of Bulldogs.

Munson